KT-559-606

30131 05516056 5

LONDON BOROUGH OF BARNET

For Pamyu Pamyu ~ MS

For Yasmine ~ SH

Bloomsbury Publishing, London, Oxford, New York, New Delhi and Sydney

First published in Great Britain in 2016 by Bloomsbury Publishing Plc
50 Bedford Square, London, WC1B 3DP

www.bloomsbury.com

BLOOMSBURY is a registered trademark of Bloomsbury Publishing Plc

Text copyright © Mark Sperring 2016
Illustrations copyright © Sue Hendra 2016
The moral rights of the author and illustrator have been asserted

All rights reserved

No part of this publication may be reproduced or
transmitted by any means, electronic, mechanical, photocopying
or otherwise, without prior permission of the publisher

A CIP catalogue record of this book is available from the British Library

ISBN 978 1 4088 6712 9 (HB)
ISBN 978 1 4088 6714 3 (PB)
ISBN 978 1 4088 6713 6 (eBook)

All papers used by Bloomsbury Publishing are natural, recyclable products made
from wood grown in well managed forests. The manufacturing processes
conform to the environmental regulations of the country of origin

Printed in China by Leo Paper Products, Heshan, Guangdong

1 3 5 7 9 10 8 6 4 2

FOUR SILLY SKELETONS

Mark Sperring

Illustrated by Sue Hendra
and Paul Linnet

BLOOMSBURY

LONDON OXFORD NEW YORK NEW DELHI SYDNEY

Belle   and Bill ....

They live in this house at the top of this STEEP hill!

And here at the bottom where the ground is good and flat,
lives their dear, sweet Auntie June and her SKELLYBONES cat.

Now, every single day there always seems to be ...

a silly little mishap, sometimes TWO or THREE ...

But luckily dear Auntie June is never far away
to pick up all the pieces and make everything OK . . .

On one DARK and STARRY night,
when the moon was big and round,
Skelly Fred heard music . . .
such a sweet TOE-TAPPING sound!

Belle, she started TWIRLING,

Bill's knees began to KNOCK.

Then "Cuckoo" went the cuckoo in the "SkellyCuckoo" clock.

"It's midnight!" shouted Skelly Sid.
"But what do we all care?
How can we think of sleeping
when there's music in the air . . ."

So, four silly skeletons shimmied down the hill with a SWISH and a SWAY and a LEAP and a TWIRL.

Rhumba, samba . . . well, look at them all go,
bone-rocking, high-kicking TO and funny FRO!

Jive-bopping, leap-frogging – oh, a body 'POP'
until a sweet, worried voice cried . . .

It was dear, sweet Auntie June, with a bottomless bag,
and she said to those skeletons, "I'm not one to nag...

...but take these lamps and torches
and this shining candlestick!
For it's dark out on this steep, STEEP hill.
You know I worry sick!"

But four silly skeletons
said they didn't need more light.
"Just look," they said to Auntie June,
"the moon's still big and bright!"

So, off they danced . . .

with a skip and a hop . . . .

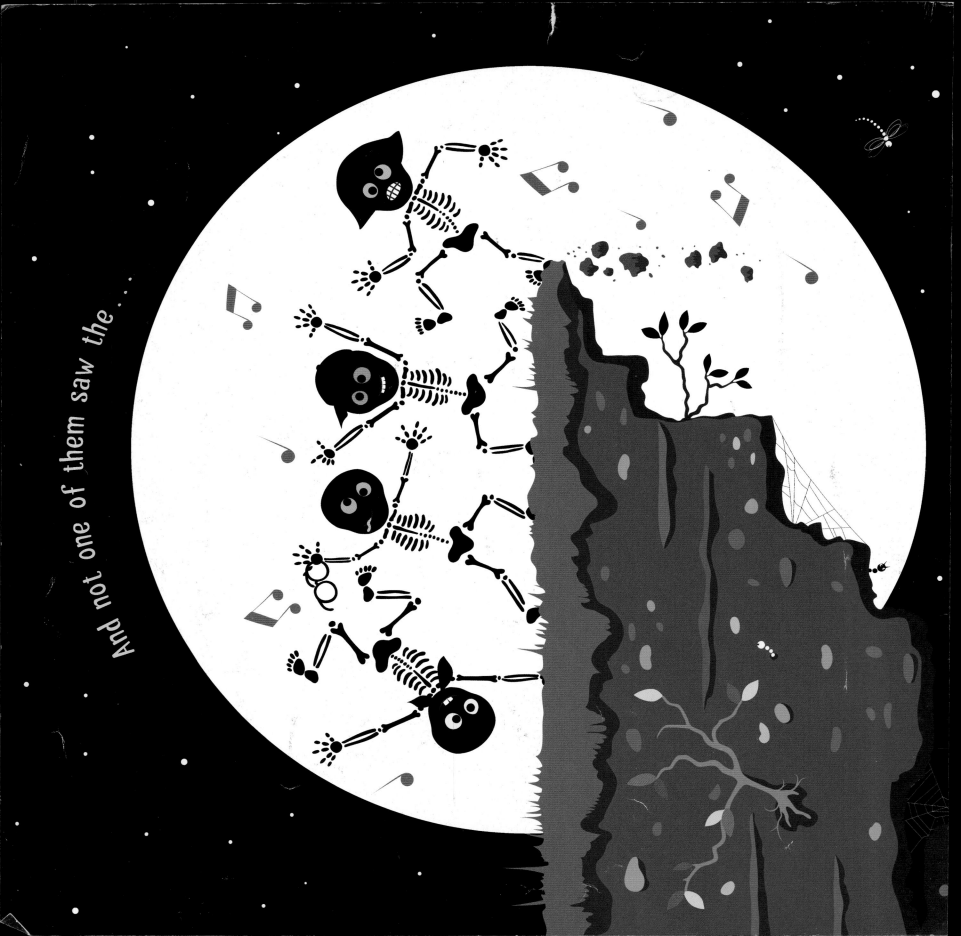

And not one of them saw the.....

Four silly skeletons all in a heap,
a pile of bones, stacked up steep!
Moaning and groaning beneath the cloudy moon,
weeping and wailing . . .

"We want our Auntie June!!"

And, just then, came a bright, beaming light
that shone like gold in the dark, dark night.

And dear Auntie June took out some string and "sticky" glue

and put them back together – almost as good as new . . .

Now Belle has two left feet,

Fred has two right,

Bill is a muddle

and Sid says,
"Serves us right."

"The next time we go dancing beneath the full moon,
we really MUST listen to clever Auntie June."